THE SUN IN MY BELLY

THE SUN

Plum Blossom Books
P.O. Box 7355
Berkeley, California 94707
www.parallax.org

Plum Blossom Books is an imprint of Parallax Press,
the publishing division of Unified Buddhist Church, Inc.

All illustrations by Sister Rain.
Design by Debbie Berne, Herter Studio LLC, San Francisco.

Library of Congress Cataloging-in-Publication Data

Susan, Sister.
  The sun in my belly / story by Sister Susan; illustrated by Sister
Rain.
     p. cm.
  Summary: Sad and lonely after a disagreement causes them to
stop playing together, Jenny and Molly find comfort in nature and
begin to understand the importance of friendship and forgiveness
and how they are connected to everything in the world around
them.
  ISBN 1-888375-64-7 (pbk.)
  [1. Friendship—Fiction. 2. Conduct of life—Fiction.] I. Rain,
Sister, ill. II. Title.
PZ7.S965645Sun 2007
  [E]—dc22

                                    2006033146

1 2 3 4 5 / 11 10 09 08 07

Story by Sister Susan

Illustrations by Sister Rain

IN MY BELLY

Inspired by the teachings of Thich Nhat Hanh

Plum
Blossom
Books
Berkeley, California

It was an early morning. The blue sky was hiding behind dark gray clouds. Jenny and her friend Molly were playing with a red ball in a meadow.

"My turn," Jenny said, throwing the ball as far as she could.

Molly ran after it. "My turn," she said, throwing the ball as far as she could.

Jenny and Molly both ran across the meadow after the ball.

"It's my turn!" said Jenny, reaching for the ball.

"No, I want another turn!" said Molly, taking the ball and running back up the meadow.

"Then I don't want to play with you anymore," said Jenny.

"Fine," said Molly, "I don't want to play with you either." She took the ball and ran away.

Jenny felt all alone in
the meadow. She sat down
against a large oak tree and
cried.

Big tears ran down her face and fell into her hands.
She cried until she couldn't feel any tears left in her.

Sitting quietly in the meadow, she felt something warm and soft touch her head.

She looked up.

The sun was coming over the mountain, lighting up the sky with rays of gold and orange.

The warmth reached all the way to her belly.

"Oh," Jenny said, surprised. "The sun is so beautiful and the sunshine has come right inside of me."

Jenny sat still and watched as the sunshine lit the trees and the green grass of the meadow. Looking down the hill, she could see the sun touching her house, making the brown roof shine.

But soon dark gray clouds moved overhead.

Jenny felt the first drops of rain on her hair.

The rain got stronger and big raindrops fell into her hands.

"The raindrops are mixing with my tears in my hands. They are both the same," she thought.

Jenny looked around and saw water everywhere. There was rain falling on the grass, the trees, and the roof of her house. The little pond was full of water too.

She knew she drank water every day, took a warm bath every night, and she remembered the tears she had just shed.

"Both the water and the sun are part of me," thought Jenny. "I can't wait to tell Molly!"

Then she remembered that she and Molly had fought.

Jenny turned to walk home across the meadow and saw Molly coming toward her with an umbrella.

Jenny and Molly stood under the umbrella together and watched the rain.

Jenny said, "I'm sorry I said I didn't want to play with you earlier."

And Molly said, "I'm sorry I didn't wait my turn. Let's be friends again."

Then Jenny said, "I think you must be inside of me, just like the sun and the raindrops."

"And you must be in me, along with the sun and the rain," said Molly. "I like having all those things inside me."

Jenny and Molly decided to go get warm and dry and have break-fast together.

As they walked quietly home, they passed a cow. Jenny looked at the cow very thoughtfully. The cow had made the milk that would be in her breakfast cereal. So the cow was part of her too.

They went past the wheat field. The wheat swayed in the wind. Soon it would be cut and made into flour for the toast that she loved to eat. So the beautiful wheat was in her too.

Jenny and Molly suddenly stopped under an apple tree. Molly helped lift her up and Jenny picked two small green apples from the lowest hanging branch. She gave one to Molly. Now the apple and the tree were inside her as well.

Jenny was quiet for a moment. She could feel her own calm breath, breathing in and breathing out.

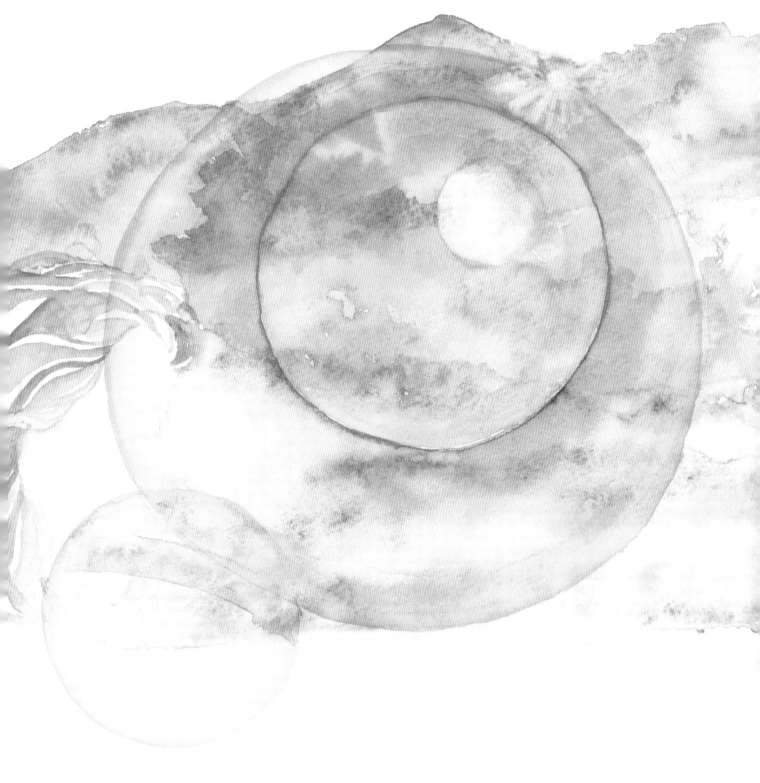

She knew she had learned something special that day. Even if no one was right next to her, Jenny would never be really alone. All the different things that were on the Earth, the people, the trees, even the air she breathed, were inside of her. Molly stood next to her and smiled. Then they both went in for breakfast.

Jenny has watched the sun come up and the sun go down many times since that day. As the sun rises in the sky, she smiles. As the sun goes down, she says, "Bye-bye, sun." She knows the sun is still inside her, even when it is dark or raining. She knows that the night and the rain are inside her as well.

Whenever Jenny is
sad, she remembers the sun
and the rain, the cow, and
the wheat, and knows she
is connected to

everything

else

in the

world.

About the Author

Sister Susan (Susan Swan), a grandmother and former teacher, was ordained as a nun in the tradition of Thich Nhat Hanh. She lives and practices at Deer Park Monastery in Escondido, California. She is very grateful for the practice and joy of mindfulness, and has the wholehearted wish that it will benefit children as well. This is her second book.

About the Illustrator

Sister Rain also lives and practices in Deer Park Monastery in Escondido, CA. She loves children and raindrops.

Plum Blossom Books

Plum Blossom Books publishes books for young people on mindfulness and
Buddhism by Thich Nhat Hanh and other authors. For a complete list of
titles for children, or a free copy of our catalog, please contact:

Plum Blossom Books
Parallax Press
www.parallax.org
P.O. Box 7355
Berkeley, CA 94707
Tel: (510) 525-0101

Practice Opportunities with Children

Individuals, families, and young people are invited to practice the art of mindful living in the tradition of Thich Nhat Hanh at retreat communities in France and the United States. For information, please visit www.plumvillage.org or contact:

Plum Village
13 Martineau
33580 Dieulivol, France
info@plumvillage.org

Green Mountain Dharma Center
P.O. Box 182
Hartland Four Corners, VT 05049
mfmaster@vermontel.net
Tel: (802) 436-1103

Deer Park Monastery
2499 Melru Lane
Escondido, CA 92026
deerpark@plumvillage.org
Tel: (760) 291-1003